W9-CBN-378

AN

Arnold Lobel
Treasury

by Arnold Lobel

Grasshopper on the Road

Owl at Home

Mouse Soup

BARNES
&NOBLE
BOOKS
NEW YORK

Reprinted by permission of HarperCollins Publishers

For Kohar Alexanian

HarperCollins®, ✎®, Harper Trophy®, and I Can Read Book®
are trademarks of HarperCollins Publishers Inc.

A portion of this book previously appeared in *Cricket*.

Grasshopper on the Road
Copyright © 1978 by Arnold Lobel
All rights reserved. No part of this book may be used or
reproduced in any manner whatsoever without written
permission except in the case of brief quotations embodied
in critical articles and reviews. Printed in the United
States of America. For information address HarperCollins
Children's Books, a division of HarperCollins Publishers,
10 East 53rd Street, New York, NY 10022.

Library of Congress Cataloging-in-Publication Data
Lobel, Arnold.
    Grasshopper on the road.

    (An I can read book)
    SUMMARY: As Grasshopper sets out to follow a road,
he meets some unusual characters.
    [1. Animals—Fiction]   I. Title
PZ7.L7795Gp 1978   [E]   77-25653
ISBN 0-06-023961-1
ISBN 0-06-023962-X (lib. bdg.)
ISBN 0-06-444094-X (pbk.)

First Harper Trophy Edition, 1986.

GRASSHOPPER
ON THE ROAD
ARNOLD LOBEL

An I Can Read Book®

■ HarperTrophy®
A Division of HarperCollins*Publishers*

CONTENTS

Grasshopper wanted

to go on a journey.

"I will find a road," he said.

"I will follow that road

wherever it goes."

One morning Grasshopper

found a road.

It was long and dusty.

It went up hills

and down into valleys.

"This road looks fine to me,"

said Grasshopper.

"I am on my way!"

The Club

Grasshopper walked quickly

along the road.

He saw a sign

on the side of a tree.

The sign said

MORNING IS BEST.

Soon Grasshopper

saw another sign.

It said

THREE CHEERS FOR MORNING.

Grasshopper saw

a group of beetles.

They were singing and dancing.

They were carrying more signs.

"Good morning,"

said Grasshopper.

"Yes," said one

of the beetles.

"It is a good morning.

Every morning

is a good morning!"

The beetle carried a sign.

It said MAKE MINE MORNING.

"This is a meeting of the

We Love Morning Club,"

said the beetle.

"Every day we get together

to celebrate

another bright, fresh morning.

10

Grasshopper,

do you love morning?"

asked the beetle.

"Oh yes," said Grasshopper.

"Hooray!" shouted all the beetles.

"Grasshopper loves morning!"

"I knew it," said the beetle.

"I could tell by your kind face.

You are a morning lover."

The beetles made Grasshopper

a wreath of flowers.

They gave him a sign that said

MORNING IS TOPS.

"Now," they said,

"Grasshopper is in our club."

"When does the clover

sparkle with dew?" asked a beetle.

"In the morning!"

 cried all the other beetles.

"When is the sunshine

yellow and new?"

asked the beetle.

"In the morning!"

cried all the other beetles.

They turned somersaults

and stood on their heads.

They danced and sang.

"M–O–R–N–I–N–G

spells morning!"

13

"I love afternoon too,"

said Grasshopper.

The beetles stopped

singing and dancing.

"What did you say?" they asked.

"I said that I loved afternoon,"

said Grasshopper.

All the beetles were quiet.

"And night is very nice,"

said Grasshopper.

"Stupid," said a beetle.

He grabbed the wreath of flowers.

"Dummy," said another beetle.

He snatched the sign

from Grasshopper.

"Anyone who loves

afternoon and night

can never, never

be in our club!"

said a third beetle.

"UP WITH MORNING!"

shouted all the beetles.

They waved their signs

and marched away.

Grasshopper was alone.

He saw the yellow sunshine.

He saw the dew

sparkling on the clover.

And he went on down the road.

A New House

The road went up a steep hill.

Grasshopper climbed to the top.

He found a large apple

lying on the ground.

"I will have my lunch,"

said Grasshopper.

He ate a big bite of the apple.

"Look what you did!" said a worm,

who lived in the apple.

"You have made a hole in my roof!"

"It is not polite

to eat a person's house,"

said the worm.

"I am sorry," said Grasshopper.

Just then the apple

began to roll down the road

on the other side of the hill.

"Stop me! Catch me!"

cried the worm.

The apple was rolling

faster and faster.

"Help, my head
is bumping on the walls!
My dishes are falling
off the shelf!"
cried the worm.

Grasshopper ran

after the apple.

"Everything is a mess in here!"

cried the worm.

"My bathtub is

in the living room.

My bed is in the kitchen!"

Grasshopper
kept running
down the hill.
But he could not catch
the apple.
"I am getting dizzy,"
cried the worm.
"My floor is on the ceiling!
My attic is in the cellar!"
The apple
rolled and rolled.
It rolled all the way down
to the bottom of the hill.

The apple hit a tree.

It smashed

into a hundred pieces.

"Too bad, worm,"

said Grasshopper.

"Your house is gone."

22

The worm
climbed up
the side
of the tree.
"Oh, never mind,"
said the worm.
"It was old,
and it had a big bite
in it anyway.
This is a fine time
for me to find a new house."

23

Grasshopper looked up
into the tree.

He saw that it was filled
with apples.

Grasshopper smiled,
and he went on down the road.

The Sweeper

Grasshopper saw

a cloud of dust.

"Clean, clean, clean,"

said a housefly,

who was sweeping the road.

"My broom and I

will make this road

as clean as can be."

"Housefly," said Grasshopper,

"the road is not very dirty."

"It is much too dusty,"
said the housefly.
"It is covered
with stones and sticks
and other nasty things.
My broom and I
will brush them all away."

26

The housefly went on sweeping.

"One day I was at home,

not doing much of anything,"

said the housefly.

"I saw a speck of dust on my rug.

I picked up the speck of dust.

Next to it was

another speck of dust.

I picked up that one, too."

"Next to that speck of dust

was another speck of dust.

I ran and got my broom.

I swept up

all the dust

that was on my rug.

28

Then I saw a piece of dirt

on my floor.

Next to it

was another piece of dirt.

And next to that

was another piece of dirt.

With my broom

I swept up all the dirt

that was on my floor."

"I cleaned my whole house

from top to bottom.

I even washed my windows.

After I washed them,

I looked outside.

I saw my garden path.

There were ugly pebbles

on my garden path.

I rushed outside with my broom.

I swept all the pebbles away.

At the end of the path

was my gate.

It was covered

with mud and moss.

I scrubbed

all the mud and moss

off my gate.

I opened the gate

and walked out onto

this dusty, dirty road."

31

"I took my broom

and went sweep, sweep, sweep

up the road," said the housefly.

"You have worked very hard,"

said Grasshopper.

"I think that you

should rest for a while."

"No, no, no," said the housefly.

"I will never rest.

I am having a wonderful time.

I will sweep

until the whole world

is clean, clean, clean!"

32

The dust was getting

into Grasshopper's eyes.

So he said good-bye

to the housefly,

and he went on

down the road.

The Voyage

Grasshopper came

to a puddle of water

in the road.

He was just about

to hop over the puddle.

"Wait!" cried a tiny voice.

Grasshopper looked down.

At the edge of the puddle

was a mosquito.

He was sitting in a little boat.

34

"It is a rule," said the mosquito.

"You must use

this ferry boat

to get across the lake."

"But sir,"

said Grasshopper,

"I can easily jump over

to the other side."

"Rules are rules,"

said the mosquito.

"Climb into my boat."

"Your boat is too small for me,"

said Grasshopper.

"Rules are rules,"

said the mosquito.

"You *must*

get into my boat!"

"I can't fit

into your boat,"

said Grasshopper.

"Rules are still rules!"

shouted the mosquito.

"Well then," said Grasshopper,

"there is only one thing

for me to do."

Grasshopper picked up the boat.

"All aboard,"

called the mosquito.

Grasshopper held the boat

very carefully.

He stepped into the puddle.

"You are lucky

to be with me

on this voyage,"

said the mosquito.

"I have been sailing
back and forth
across this lake
for many years,"
said the mosquito.
"I am not afraid
of storms or waves."
Grasshopper took another step.

"I know more

about sailing

than anyone else around here,"

said the mosquito.

Grasshopper took

one more step.

He was on

the other side

of the puddle.

He put the boat

down into the water.

"That was a good trip,"
said the mosquito.
"Now I must hurry back
to the other shore
to wait for new riders."

41

"Thank you," said Grasshopper.

"Thank you very much

for taking me

safely across the lake."

"I was glad to do it,"

said the mosquito.

Grasshopper waved good-bye

and kept on

walking down the road.

Always

In the late afternoon

Grasshopper saw a mushroom.

It was growing

at the edge of the road.

"I will rest my feet," he said.

Grasshopper sat on the mushroom.

Three butterflies flew down.

"Grasshopper,"

said the butterflies,

"you will have to move."

"Yes," said the first butterfly.

"You are sitting on our place.

Every afternoon at this time,

we fly to this mushroom.

We sit down on it for a while."

"There are lots of other mushrooms,"

said Grasshopper.

"They will not do,"

said the second butterfly.

"This is the mushroom

we *always* sit on."

Grasshopper got up.

The three butterflies sat down.

"Each and every day

we do the same thing

at the same time,"

said the third butterfly.

"We like it that way."

"We wake up in the morning,"

said the first butterfly.

"We scratch our heads three times."

Always," said the second butterfly.

Then we open and close our wings

our times.

Ve fly in a circle six times."

Always," said the third butterfly.

We go to the same tree

nd eat the same lunch every day."

"Always," said the first butterfly.

"After lunch we sit

on the same sunflower.

We take the same nap.

We have the same dream.

"What sort of dream?"

asked Grasshopper.

"We dream that

we are sitting

on a sunflower

taking a nap,"

said the second

butterfly.

"Always," said the third butterfly.

"When we wake up,

we scratch our heads

three more times.

We fly in a circle six more times."

"Then we come here,"

said the first butterfly.

"We sit down on *this* mushroom."

"Always," said the second butterfly.

"Don't you ever change anything?"

asked Grasshopper.

"No, never," said the butterflies.

"Each day is fine for us."

"Grasshopper,"

said the butterflies,

"we like talking to you.

We will meet you

every day at this time.

We will sit on this mushroom.

You will sit right there.

We will tell you all about

our scratching and our flying.

We will tell you all about

our napping and our dreaming.

You will listen just the way

you are listening now."

51

"No," said Grasshopper.

"I am sorry,

but I will not be here.

I will be moving on.

I will be doing new things."

"That is too bad,"

said the butterflies.

"We will miss you.

Grasshopper, do you really

do something *different*

every day of your life?"

"Always," said Grasshopper.

"Always and always!"

He said good-bye

to the butterflies

and walked quickly

down the road.

At Evening

In the evening

Grasshopper walked slowly

along the road.

The sun was going down.

The world was soft and quiet.

Grasshopper heard

a loud sound.

ZOOM!

Grasshopper heard

another noise.

ZOOOM!

He saw two dragonflies

in the air.

"Poor Grasshopper,"

said the dragonflies.

"We are flying fast.

You are only walking.

That is very sad."

"It is not sad,"

said Grasshopper.

"I like to walk."

The dragonflies flew
over Grasshopper's head.
"We can see so many things
from up here,"
said the dragonflies.
"All you can see
is that road."
"I like this road,"
said Grasshopper.
"And I can see
flowers growing
along the side of the road."

56

"We are zipping

and zooming,"

said the first dragonfly.

"We do not have time

to look at flowers."

"I can see leaves

moving in the trees,"

said Grasshopper.

"We are looping

and spinning,"

said the second dragonfly.

"We do not have time

to look at leaves."

"I can see the sunset

over the mountains,"

said Grasshopper.

"What sunset?

What mountains?"

asked the dragonflies.

"We are diving and dipping.

There is no time

to look at sunsets and mountains."

ZOOOOM!

The two dragonflies

raced across the sky.

Soon they were gone.

The world was quiet again.

The sky became dark.

Grasshopper watched the moon

rising over the land.

He watched the stars come out.

He was happy

to be walking slowly

down the road.

Grasshopper was tired.

He lay down in a soft place.

He knew that in the morning

the road would still be there,

taking him on and on

to wherever

he wanted to go.

An I Can Read Book®

OWL AT HOME

by ARNOLD LOBEL

An I CAN READ Book®

HarperTrophy®
A Division of HarperCollins*Publishers*

For Grandma

HarperCollins®, ♠®, Harper Trophy®, and I Can Read Book®
are trademarks of HarperCollins Publishers Inc.

A portion of this book previously appeared in *Cricket*.

Owl at Home

Copyright © 1975 by Arnold Lobel
All rights reserved. No part of this book may be used or reproduced in any
manner whatsoever without written permission except in the case of brief
quotations embodied in critical articles and reviews. Printed in the United
States of America. For information address HarperCollins Children's
Books, a division of HarperCollins Publishers, 10 East 53rd Street,
New York, NY 10022.

Library of Congress Catalog Card Number: 74-2630
ISBN 0-06-023948-4
ISBN 0-06-023949-2 (lib. bdg.)
ISBN 0-06-444034-6 (pbk.)

First Harper Trophy edition, 1982.

CONTENTS

THE GUEST

Owl was at home.

"How good it feels

to be sitting

by this fire," said Owl.

"It is so cold

and snowy outside."

Owl was eating

buttered toast

and hot pea soup

for supper.

5

Owl heard a loud sound

at the front door.

"Who is out there,

banging and pounding

at my door

on a night like this?"

he said.

Owl opened the door.

No one was there.

Only the snow

and the wind.

Owl sat near the fire again.

There was another loud noise

at the door.

"Who can it be," said Owl,

"knocking and thumping

at my door on a night like this?"

Owl opened the door.

No one was there.

Only the snow

and the cold.

"The poor old winter

is knocking at my door,"

said Owl.

"Perhaps it wants to sit

by the fire.

Well, I will be kind

and let the winter come in."

Owl opened his door very wide.

"Come in, Winter,"

said Owl.

"Come in and warm yourself

for a while."

Winter came into the house.

It came in very fast.

A cold wind

pushed Owl against the wall.

10

Winter ran around the room.

It blew out the fire

in the fireplace.

11

The snow whirled

up the stairs

and whooshed down the hallway.

"Winter!" cried Owl.

"You are my guest.

This is no way to behave!"

But Winter did not listen.

It made the window shades

flap and shiver.

It turned the pea soup

into hard, green ice.

Winter went into all the rooms

of Owl's house.

Soon everything

was covered with snow.

"You must go, Winter!"

shouted Owl.

"Go away, right now!"

14

The wind blew

around and around.

Then Winter rushed out

and slammed the front door.

"Good-bye," called Owl,

"and do not come back!"

Owl made a new fire

in the fireplace.

The room became

warm again.

The snow melted away.

The hard, green ice

turned back

into soft pea soup.

Owl sat down in his chair

and quietly

finished his supper.

STRANGE BUMPS

Owl was in bed.

"It is time

to blow out the candle

and go to sleep,"

he said with a yawn.

Then Owl saw two bumps

under the blanket

at the bottom of his bed.

"What can those strange bumps

be?" asked Owl.

Owl lifted up the blanket.

He looked down into the bed.

All he could see was darkness.

Owl tried to sleep,

but he could not.

20

"What if those

two strange bumps

grow bigger and bigger

while I am asleep?"

said Owl.

"That would not be pleasant."

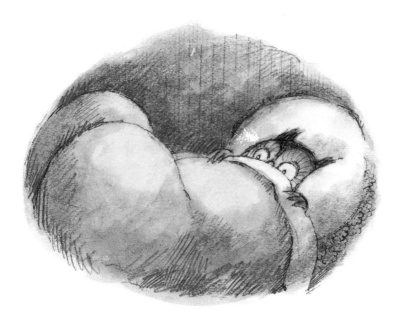

Owl moved his right foot

up and down.

The bump on the right

moved up and down.

"One of those bumps

is moving!" said Owl.

Owl moved his left foot

up and down.

The bump

on the left

moved up and down.

"The other bump is moving!"

cried Owl.

Owl pulled

all of the covers

off his bed.

The bumps were gone.

All Owl could see

at the bottom of the bed

were his own two feet.

23

"But now I am cold,"

said Owl.

"I will cover myself

with the blankets again."

As soon as he did,

he saw the same two bumps.

"Those bumps are back!"

shouted Owl.

"Bumps, bumps, bumps!

I will never sleep tonight!"

Owl jumped

up and down

on top of his bed.

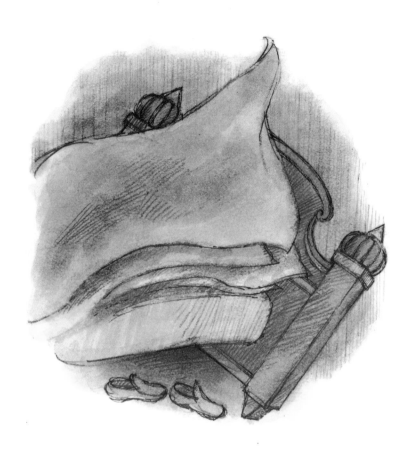

"Where are you?

What are you?" he cried.

With a crash and a bang

the bed came falling down.

Owl ran
down the stairs.
He sat in his chair
near the fire.
"I will let those two strange bumps
sit on my bed
all by themselves,"
said Owl.
"Let them grow
as big as they wish.
I will sleep right here
where I am safe."

28

And that is what he did.

29

TEAR-WATER TEA

Owl took the kettle

out of the cupboard.

"Tonight I will make

tear-water tea," he said.

He put the kettle on his lap.

"Now," said Owl,

"I will begin."

Owl sat very still.

He began to think of

things that were sad.

"Chairs with broken legs,"

said Owl.

His eyes

began to water.

"Songs that cannot be sung,"

said Owl,

"because the words

have been forgotten."

Owl began to cry.

A large tear

rolled down

and dropped

into the kettle.

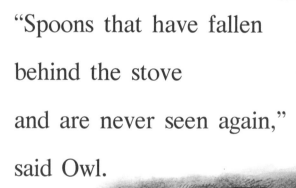

"Spoons that have fallen

behind the stove

and are never seen again,"

said Owl.

More tears dropped down

into the kettle.

"Books that cannot
be read," said Owl,
"because some of the pages
have been torn out."

"Clocks that have stopped,"
said Owl,
"with no one near
to wind them up."

Owl was crying.

Many large tears

dropped into the kettle.

"Mornings nobody saw

because everybody

was sleeping,"

sobbed Owl.

"Mashed potatoes

left on a plate," he cried,

"because no one

wanted to eat them.

And pencils

that are too short to use."

Owl thought about

many other sad things.

He cried and cried.

Soon the kettle

was all filled up

with tears.

37

"There," said Owl.

"That does it!"

Owl stopped crying.

He put the kettle

on the stove

to boil for tea.

38

Owl felt happy

as he filled his cup.

"It tastes

a little bit salty,"

he said,

"but tear-water tea

is always very good."

UPSTAIRS AND DOWNSTAIRS

Owl's house had an upstairs
and a downstairs.
There were twenty steps
on the stairway.
Some of the time
Owl was upstairs
in his bedroom.
At other times
Owl was downstairs
in his living room.

When Owl was downstairs

he said, "I wonder

how my upstairs is?"

When Owl was upstairs

he said, "I wonder

how my downstairs

is getting along?

I am always missing

one place or the other.

There must be a way," said Owl,

"to be upstairs

and to be downstairs

at the same time."

42

'Perhaps if I run

very very fast,

I can be

in both places at once."

Owl ran up

the stairs.

'I am up," he said.

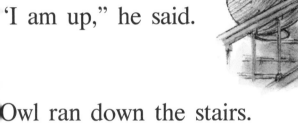

Owl ran down the stairs.

"I am down,"

he said.

Owl ran

up and down

the stairs

faster and faster.

"Owl!" he cried.

"Are you downstairs?"

There was no answer.

"No," said Owl.

"I am not downstairs

because I am upstairs.

I am not running fast enough."

44

"Owl!" he shouted.

"Are you upstairs?"

There was no answer.

"No," said Owl.

"I am not upstairs

because I am downstairs.

I must run even faster."

"Faster, faster, faster!"

cried Owl.

Owl ran upstairs

and downstairs

all evening.

But he could not be

in both places at once.

47

"When I am up," said Owl,

"I am not down.

When I am down

I am not up.

All I am is very tired!"

Owl sat down to rest.

He sat on the tenth step

because it was a place

that was

right in the middle.

OWL AND THE MOON

One night

Owl went down

to the seashore.

He sat on a large rock

and looked out at the waves.

Everything was dark.

Then a small tip

of the moon

came up

over the edge of the sea.

Owl watched the moon.

It climbed higher and higher

into the sky.

Soon the whole, round moon

was shining.

Owl sat on the rock

and looked up at the moon

for a long time.

"If I am looking

at you, moon,

then you must be

looking back at me.

We must be

very good friends."

The moon did not answer,

but Owl said,

"I will come back

and see you again, moon.

But now I must go home."

Owl walked down the path.

He looked up at the sky.

The moon was still there.

It was following him.

"No, no, moon," said Owl.

"It is kind of you

to light my way.

But you must stay up

over the sea

where you look so fine."

Owl walked on a little farther.

He looked at the sky again.

There was the moon

coming right along with him.

"Dear moon," said Owl,

"you really must not

come home with me.

My house is small.

You would not fit

through the door.

And I have nothing

to give you for supper."

Owl kept on walking.

The moon

sailed after him

over the tops of the trees.

"Moon," said Owl,

"I think that

you do not hear me."

Owl climbed

to the top of a hill.

He shouted

as loudly as he could,

"Good-bye, moon!"

The moon went behind some clouds.

Owl looked and looked.

The moon was gone.

"It is always

a little sad

to say good-bye to a friend,"

said Owl.

Owl came home.

He put on his pajamas
and went to bed.

The room was very dark.

Owl was still feeling sad.

All at once,

Owl's bedroom

was filled with silver light.

Owl looked out of the window.

The moon was coming

from behind the clouds.

"Moon, you have followed me

all the way home.

What a good, round friend

you are!" said Owl.

Then Owl put his head

on the pillow

and closed his eyes.

The moon was shining

down through the window.

Owl did not

feel sad at all.

An I Can Read Book®

MOUSE SOUP

BY ARNOLD LOBEL

HarperTrophy®
A Division of HarperCollins*Publishers*

HarperCollins®, ☕®, Harper Trophy®, and I Can Read Book®
are trademarks of HarperCollins Publishers Inc.

Mouse Soup
Copyright © 1977 by Arnold Lobel
All rights reserved. No part of this book may be used or
reproduced in any manner whatsoever without written
permission except in the case of brief quotations embodied
in critical articles and reviews. Printed in the United
States of America. For information address HarperCollins
Children's Books, a division of HarperCollins Publishers,
10 East 53rd Street, New York, NY 10022.
First Harper Trophy edition, 1983.

Library of Congress Cataloging-in-Publication Data
Lobel, Arnold.
  Mouse soup.
  (An I can read book)
  SUMMARY: A mouse convinces a weasel he needs the
ingredients from several stories to make a tasty mouse soup.
  [1. Mice—Fiction] I. Title.
PZ7.L7795Mo   [E]   76-41517
ISBN 0-06-023967-0
ISBN 0-06-023968-9 (lib. bdg.)
ISBN 0-06-444041-9 (pbk.)

MOUSE SOUP

THE STORIES FOR THE SOUP

A mouse

sat under a tree.

He was reading a book.

A weasel

jumped out

and caught the mouse.

The weasel

took the mouse home.

"Ah!" said the weasel.

"I am going to make

mouse soup."

"Oh!" said the mouse.

"I am going to *be*

mouse soup."

The weasel put the mouse

in a cooking pot.

"*WAIT!*" said the mouse.

"This soup will not taste good.

It has no stories in it.

Mouse soup must be mixed

with stories

to make it taste really good."

10

"But I have no stories,"

said the weasel.

"I do," said the mouse.

"I can tell them now."

"All right," said the weasel.

"But hurry. I am very hungry."

"Here are four stories

to put in the soup," said the mouse.

BEES AND THE MUD

A mouse was walking

through the woods.

A nest of bees

fell from a tree.

It landed on the top of his head.

"Bees," said the mouse,

"you will have to fly away.

I do not want a nest of bees

sitting on the top

of my head."

13

But the bees said,

"We like your ears,

we like your nose,

we like your whiskers.

Oh yes, this is a fine place

for our nest.

We will never fly away."

The mouse was upset.

He did not know

what to do.

The buzzing of the bees

was very loud.

The mouse walked on.

He came to a muddy swamp.

"Bees," said the mouse,

"I have a nest like yours.

It is my home.

If you want to stay on my head,

you will have to

come home with me."

"Oh yes," said the bees.

"We like your ears,

we like your nose,

we like your whiskers.

We will be glad

to come home with you."

"Very well," said the mouse.

He stepped into the mud

up to his knees.

"Here is my front door,"

said the mouse.

"Oh yes," said the bees.

The mouse

stepped into the mud

up to his waist.

"Here is my living room,"

said the mouse.

"Oh yes," said the bees.

The mouse

stepped into the mud

up to his chin.

"Here is my bedroom,"

said the mouse.

"Oh yes," said the bees.

"And now I will go to sleep,"

said the mouse.

He ducked his head

under the mud.

"Oh no!" said the bees.

"We like your front door.

We like your living room.

We like your bedroom.

But no, no, no,

we do not like your bed!"

The bees jumped up into the air

and flew away.

The mouse went home

to take a bath.

TWO LARGE STONES

Two large stones

sat on the side of a hill.

Grass and flowers grew there.

"This side of the hill

is nice,"

said the first stone.

"But I wonder

what is on

the other side

of the hill?"

"We do not know.

We never will,"

said the second stone.

One day

a bird flew down.

"Bird, can you tell us

what is on the other side

of the hill?"

asked the stones.

The bird flew up into the sky.

He flew high over the hill.

He came back and said,

"I can see towns and castles.

I can see mountains

and valleys.

It is a wonderful sight."

The first stone said,

"All of those things

are on the other side

of the hill."

"How sad,"

said the second stone.

"We cannot see them.

We never will."

The two stones

sat on the side of the hill.

They felt sad

for one hundred years.

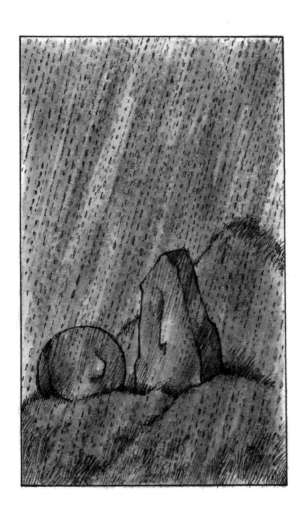

One day

a mouse walked by.

"Mouse, can you tell us

what is on the other side

of the hill?"

asked the stones.

The mouse climbed up the hill.

He put his nose over the top
and looked down.

He came back and said,

"I can see earth and stones.

I can see grass and flowers.

It is a wonderful sight."

The first stone said,

"The bird

told us a lie.

That side of the hill

looks just the same

as this side

of the hill."

"Oh good!"

said the second stone.

"We feel happy now.

We always will."

THE CRICKETS

One night a mouse woke up.

There was a chirping sound

outside her window.

"What is that noise?"

asked the mouse.

"What did you say?"

asked a cricket.

"I cannot hear you

and make my music

at the same time."

"I want to sleep,"

said the mouse.

"I do not want

any more music."

"What did you say?"

asked the cricket.

"You want more music?

I will find a friend."

Soon there were

two crickets chirping.

"I want you

to stop the music,"

said the mouse.

"You are giving me more!"

"What did you say?"

asked the cricket.

"You want more music?

We will find another friend."

Soon there were

three crickets chirping.

"You must stop the music,"

said the mouse.

"I am tired.

I cannot take much more!"

"What did you say?"

asked the cricket.

"You want much more music?

We will find

many friends."

Soon there were

ten crickets chirping.

"Stop!" cried the mouse.

"Your music

is too loud!"

"Loud?" asked the cricket.

"Yes, we can chirp loud."

So the ten crickets

chirped

very loud.

"Please!" shouted the mouse.

"I want to sleep.

I wish that you would all

"Go away?" asked the cricket.

"Why didn't you say so

in the first place?"

"We will go away

and chirp somewhere else,"

said the ten crickets.

They went away

and chirped somewhere else.

And the mouse went back to sleep.

THE THORN BUSH

An old lady

went to the door

of her house.

She was crying.

A policeman came running.

"Dear lady,"

said the policeman,

"why are you crying?"

"Come in," said the old lady.

"I will show you."

"Look, there is
a thorn bush
growing in
my living-room chair,"
said the old lady.

"How did it get there?"

asked the policeman.

"I do not know,"

said the old lady.

"One day I sat down

and something hurt me.

I got up.

There was the thorn bush."

"You poor lady,"

said the policeman.

"I will pull the thorn bush

out of your chair.

Then you can sit down again."

"No!" cried the old lady.

"Don't do that!

I do not want to sit down.

I have been sitting down

all my life.

I love my thorn bush.

I am crying because it is sick.

See?" said the old lady.

"All of the branches

are falling over."

"The thorn bush

may be thirsty,"

said the policeman.

"Perhaps it needs water."

"I never thought of that,"

said the old lady.

She poured some water

on the chair.

The thorn bush

shivered and shook.

Green leaves came out

on the branches.

Little buds came out

near the leaves.

The buds opened up.

They became large roses.

"Thank you, kind policeman!"

cried the old lady.

"You have saved

my thorn bush!

You have made

my house beautiful!"

She kissed the policeman

and gave him a big bunch

of roses to take home.

"There," said the mouse.

"I have told you my stories.

They will make your mouse soup

taste really good."

"All right," said the weasel,

"but how can I

put the stories into the soup?"

"That will be easy,"

said the mouse.

"Run outside and find

a nest of bees,

some mud,

two large stones,

ten crickets,

and a thorn bush.

Come back

and put them

all into the soup."

The weasel ran outside

very fast.

He forgot to close the door.

The weasel found

a nest of bees.

He was stung many times.

The weasel found

some mud.

It was wet and gooey.

The weasel found

two large stones.

They were heavy.

The weasel found

ten crickets.

He had to jump

to catch them.

The weasel found

a thorn bush.

He was pricked

and scratched.

"Now my mouse soup

will taste really good!"

said the weasel.

But when the weasel

came back to his house,

he found a surprise.

The cooking pot was empty.

The mouse hurried

to his safe home.

He lit the fire,

he ate his supper,

and he finished

reading his book.